To Lilly, who would likely want to keep any cute critter who followed her home
—Rebecca

To Rachel, for believing in me
—Larissa

Center for Responsive Schools, Inc.,
is a not-for-profit educational organization.

First edition, June 2019
10 9 8 7 6 5 4 3

Written by Rebecca Roan
Illustrated by Larissa Marantz
Edited by Sera Rivers
Book design by Liz Brandenburg and Hannah Collins
Printed in the United States of America

ISBN: 978-1-950317-00-4
Library of Congress Control Number: 2019935323

Avenue A Books
An imprint of
Center for Responsive Schools, Inc.
85 Avenue A, P.O. Box 718
Turners Falls, MA 01376-0718
800-360-6332
avenueabooks.org
crslearn.org

CHARLIE
and the
OCTOPUS

Rebecca Roan • **Larissa Marantz**

Charlie went to the aquarium.

And he came home with an octopus.

2

No, not that one. He already had that one.

Yes, that's the one.

But it took a while for Charlie to notice.

Charlie did his homework.

He practiced on the piano.

He played a board game.

He had dinner with his family.

He was hungrier than he thought.

He got ready for bed.

AAAAH!

And that was when Charlie noticed something was different.

What's wrong, Charlie?

It's an octopus!

Charlie's parents looked at him.

They looked at the octopus.
Except they were looking at
the wrong octopus.

Goodnight, Charlie.

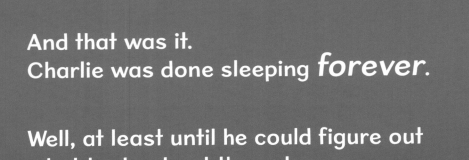

And that was it.
Charlie was done sleeping *forever*.

Well, at least until he could figure out
what to do about the octopus.

10

The octopus, on the other hand, seemed quite cozy indeed.

The next morning, Charlie dragged himself out of bed.

His stomach grumbled. So did the octopus's.

That gave Charlie an idea.

But the octopus was a rather picky eater.

It went to find
something else to eat.

Charlie! What have you done to the kitchen?!

It wasn't me! It was the octopus!

Charlie's parents looked at him.

They looked at the octopus.

Except they were looking at the wrong octopus.

Charlie needed a new plan. And he needed a bath.
So did the octopus. That gave Charlie an idea.

Charlie had the octopus right where he wanted it.
There was no way his parents could miss it now.

But nothing is **ever** that simple.

Charlie . . .

What have you done to the bathroom?!

It wasn't me! It was the octopus!

Charlie's parents looked at him.

They looked at the octopus.

And just as before,
they were not happy.

Charlie was tired of the octopus.

It had to go. But how?

And that's when Charlie had an idea.

Charlie found a box and wrote his best letters on it.

Then he | put the octopus | in the box.

Charlie's parents looked at him. They looked at the octopus. And this time, they were looking at the right octopus.

It's a **real** octopus!

AAAAH!

Charlie waved goodbye to his new friend.
He was glad the octopus was back where it belonged.
But he promised to come back and visit it soon.

He just didn't know how soon that would be ...